CLASS
DISMISSED II

CLASS DISMISSED II

MORE HIGH SCHOOL POEMS

by *MEL GLENN*

photographs by Michael J. Bernstein

CLARION BOOKS
TICKNOR & FIELDS: A HOUGHTON MIFFLIN COMPANY
NEW YORK

To Joanne E. Bernstein

Acknowledgment
The photographer thanks the young people who agreed
to be the models for the photographs in this book.

Clarion Books
Ticknor & Fields, a Houghton Mifflin Company
Text copyright © 1986 by Mel Glenn
Photographs copyright © 1986 by Michael J. Bernstein

Library of Congress Cataloging in Publication Data
Glenn, Mel.   Class Dismissed II.
Continues: Class dismissed!
Summary: Another seventy poems about the emotional
lives of contemporary high school students.
1. Children's poetry, American.   [1. High schools —
Poetry,   2. Schools — Poetry.   3. American poetry]
I. Bernstein, Michael J., ill.   II. Title.
PS3557.L447U5 1986   811'.54   86-2671
ISBN 0-89919-443-5

Q 10 9 8 7 6 5 4 3 2 1

Author's Note

The characters in this book are fictional composites of the many students I have taught through the years. Stacey, Barry, Elizabeth, and all the others live on these pages, not in real life. Yet any resemblance to actual persons is purely intentional in the artistic sense.

Contents

Stacey Fowler

My mother told me that boys are supposed to
    make the first move.
But what does she know, anyway, about hunks?
So I decided to stalk Mark
And find out everything I could about him,
His address,
His class schedule,
What friends he hung out with.
My girl friend Melanie told me what rock group
    he likes.
I even went to their concert
Just on the chance *he* might be there,
Also to buy a T-shirt so he'd notice me.
The next day in school he noticed me all right.
"Hey, Stace," he smiled, "nice shirt."
He walked right past me
And asked Melanie out.
It's gonna be some time
Before I make another move.

Barry Owens

God help me!
In the future
I'll have to
> Borrow my little brother's tricycle,
> Steal my sister's dirt bike,
> Buy shoes with thick soles,
> Flag down a cab,
> Grab on to the back of a bus,
> Run to catch the train,
> Find my old skateboard,
> Hire a camel,
> Charter a seaplane,
> Ride the waves.

I failed my road test – again!

Veronica Castell

I have seen schools in seven different states
Courtesy of the air force, which insists
    on transferring
The Colonel, my father, every two years or so.
I'm never in any school long enough to get bored.
South Carolina, Kansas, Utah,
Stopping places of the mind
Connected by a ribbon of happy memories.
My father and I singing country songs
    into the night
As our car whizzes past lit signs that say,
"You are now entering. . . ."
"You are now leaving. . . ."
He pilots;
I navigate the red lines on our Rand McNally.
Just my father and me,
My father and me.

Dana Moran

I was in such a hurry to get out of school
That I took a shortcut.
I dropped out.
Now I work full-time at the local K Mart
Putting out stock,
Handling the register,
Dealing with the crazy customers
Who hassle me about returns,
Who cut the line,
Who think I cheat them by ringing up
      the wrong prices.
Taking stock of what I've done
I see that the shelves of my life are kinda empty,
Bare, in fact.
When will it register that
There are no express lines to happiness?
I am such a fool.
Check it out.

Dorothy Osmond

Here, Dana, let me show you my room.
It's all color-coordinated, you know.
Didn't my father do a great job
      with the wallpaper?
Pink and white are my absolute favorite colors.
Don't you think so?
And I just got lace curtains last week.
Aren't they neat?
I can see the whole park from here,
The trees, the leaves, the ducks on the lake.
How many stuffed animals do I have?
Oh, I don't know.
But Puffin here is my favorite.
Isn't he cute?
I could stay in my room forever.
Let's see – there's my portable TV,
      my AM/FM radio,
My stereo, my Sony Walkman, my VCR,
      my walk-in closet,
My vanity table, my phone, my . . .
Hey, Dana, you goin' home now?

José Cruz

75 lbs. — Get serious.
100 lbs. — A little better.
125 lbs. — Now you're talkin'.
150 lbs. — I can do it.
Whenever I feel the weight of the world
On my shoulders, I go to the gym and work out.
It makes me feel good about myself.
When I crouch to snatch the bar,
I don't think about nothin' else
'Cept puttin' it over my head.
I don't think about
School,
My life,
My future,
Nothin'.
Put on more weights.
I can handle it, man.
No sweat.

Robert Ashford

"Harvard's nice."
"Yale's not too shabby either."
"Maybe he should go to my alma mater.
I didn't turn out so badly."
"Maybe he should go upstate like
    my sister Ellen did.
She's very successful now, you know."
"I can see him at an Ivy League school."
"I can see him at a smaller place,
    perhaps out West."
"You know, I remember when I applied to college –
I didn't have so many choices."
"Neither did I. I feel seventeen again."

"Bobby, come here.
We've narrowed it down to five choices for you."

My parents pore over my college catalogs
As if they were picking out a summer camp for me.
Sometimes I wonder who's going to college.
Me or them?

Paul Hewitt

Please, sir, I don't mean to be disrespectful.
I did raise my hand.
I mean, who cares if Macbeth becomes a monster,
If Huck Finn rescues Jim,
If Willie Loman never finds happiness?
They're just characters in books.
What have they got to do with me?
I mean, I'm never going hunting for white whales.
I'm never going to fight in the Civil War.
And I certainly don't live in the Dust Bowl.
Tell me instead how to
Make money, pick up girls.
Then maybe I'll listen.
You got any books that deal with real life?

Nolan Davis

I stepped in front of the fun house mirror
In the local amusement park.
My face contorted,
My body elongated,
My legs distorted,
All parts of me pulled in various directions
By people who say they know what's best for me.
Parents, teachers, friends
Shout advice from every corner of the park,
But all I hear is the same tinny music
Over and over again.
I wonder if I'll ever see
A clear image of myself.

Vinnie Robustelli

Her body, smooth and sleek, stands
Glistening in the moonlight.
I love it when she purrs at night
When I touch her.
I really turn her on,
Not that it takes that much to get her started.
She drives me crazy,
Taking me to places I've never been before.
She seductively whispers to me before we park,
Promising a night of new thrills.
She is
      responsive,
      elegant,
      hard-driving
      and forgiving.
I will never have another one like her.
She's my first one, something really special.
      Hey, Kevin, what are you looking at me
        like that for?
      You think I'm talking about my girl friend?
      No way, man.
      I'm telling you about my new wheels.

Mary Gilardi

I don't know how or if to get out of it.
I mean, I've been going with Vinnie so long
It's like we're married or something.
My mother adores him.
My little sister worships him.
My father admires him.
Everybody's crazy about him,
Everybody but me.
When I'm alone, I wonder if it's the real thing.
Instead of enjoying romantic dinners for two,
We watch movies on my VCR.
Instead of talking about our relationship,
We hang out with his friends.
There has to be more to life
Than Saturday night wrestling matches
In his new car.
I'm not ready to be pinned
Or pinned down, for that matter.
Yet he is sweet; everybody says so.
And I do love him.
I guess.

Nicole Harris

If it wasn't for me, Jimmy,
You'd still be out on the streets.
Who got you to go to class?
Who did your homework for you?
Me, that's who, you bastard.
Now you tell me you want your freedom?
Fat chance.
You've had your freedom all your life
And look what you've done with it.
Two of your sleazeball friends are dead,
And the rest drink themselves blind all day.
And I don't have that much hope for you.
You want to play? You want to run?
See how far you get without me.
Get real, Jimmy,
You're such a baby,
A child really.
I should throw you out of my life for good.
But I can't.
You're still my man.

Juan Pedro Carrera

To leave my home country
Made me much desponded.
You must be strong, my father told me.
Difficult that is to be when
Food is strange,
Language is strange,
Students is strange.
They speak loud to me.
I am not deaf,
Just un-understanding of the language.
I have eighteen years, but in this new country
I feel the baby, who cannot walk rightly.
Play sports, my father recommended me.
But I do not know the rules of anything
How they play in America.
I wish all the time to go back to my home country
Where I do not have to act so strong.

Jay Stone

I read the papers all the time.
I know that people are
Starving in Africa,
Fighting in the Mid-East,
Dying in Central America.
But I got my own problems.
There's nothing but leftovers in the fridge.
My father and I had it out over my grades.
If I don't get the car tonight,
My social life is history.
The world stinks.

Craig Blanchard

Because I had failing grades in history,
Because my father threatened loss of limb
    and other minor inconveniences,
Because my teacher thought I had the
    intelligence of an advanced flea,
I stayed in my room and in the library
And worked on this fantastic paper on
The Great Depression and the New Deal.
I felt in sympathy with Roosevelt
As he tried to put the country back together,
As I was trying to put my life back together.
When I turned in the paper, I felt proud of myself.
When I got it back, I felt crushed.
My history teacher had written,
"I don't think you did this by yourself.
It's too good."
The Depression isn't historical, it's personal.

Candie Brewer

At the rock club where I hang out,
I've heard every line in the book:
 Don't I know you from someplace?
 Do you come here often?
 Do you want a drink?
Or
 Would you like to dance?
 Would you like some meaningful company?
 Would you like to bear my child?
Or
 I think you're gorgeous.
 I've been watching you for hours.
 I think you're an Aries – right?
At the rock club where I hang out,
I hear every line, but just
One note.

Louise Coyle

My mother, living in the past tense,
Has kept every school report I've ever written,
Also every tooth I've lost, every award I've won.
At least once a week, she
Takes out the family photo albums
And conducts a walking tour across the
Cellophaned pages, across the years.
She has frozen me in time,
A still-life picture
In the gold-locket chamber of her heart.
Mama, I want to get out of high school,
Get out of the house,
Get out of the past.
I don't want to be ten years old forever.
I want to have my own apartment
And when I do, I'll call you regularly, I promise.
I'll even come over for dinner,
At least once a week.
And we'll look at the old pictures together.

Greg Hoffman

Lap 1 Swimming . . . . laps
2 Is . . . . such
3 A . . . . pain,
4 I . . . . wonder
5 If . . . . Coach
6 Ramsey . . . . would
7 Mind . . . . if
8 I . . . . just
9 Stopped . . . . in
10 The . . . . . . middle.

Elizabeth McKenzie

Late at night and in secret
So as to avoid stupid questions
From insensitive friends
And questioning parents,
I wrote a play in two acts.
I was afraid to show it to my English teacher,
Afraid he wouldn't like any of it
And would rip it apart,
Afraid he'd like it so much that
He wouldn't criticize it at all.
For days I circled his desk after class
And talked to him about everything except
My play.
When my ramblings became longer
And his replies more curtly polite,
I stopped going up to his desk.
Instead, I took my play home
And stuffed it in a bottom drawer
With the clothes I no longer wear.
Maybe, one day, I'll have the courage to
Get my acts together.

Justin Faust

I know that a divorce is supposed to be
    no big deal these days.
Try telling that to my mother, who
    still sometimes sets the table for three.
Try telling that to my father, who
    calls daily, "to keep in touch," he says.
My mother's not happy because I'm not happy.
I'm not happy because my mother's not happy.
A circle of pain surrounds empty evenings
And long weekends.
My mother still cries alone at night.
I hear her.
My father fights his tears over the telephone.
I hear him.
I speak to both of them practically every day.
I wish they would speak to each other.

Marcy Mannes

Dear Dad,
    I found your address, the one Mom hid from me
    In her drawer, under her sweaters
    Near where she keeps her birth control pills.
    (Don't worry, the pills are hers, not mine.)
    She's out on a date
       with some new guy from work.
    He picked her up a half hour ago.
    Before she left, she whispered
    That she wants me to stay up late
    So that when the guy brings her back
    He doesn't try anything funny.
    Sometimes,
    No, all the time,
    I wish you would appear again at the door and
    Take her out on a real date.
    Then I'd go to sleep early.

                      Love,
                      Marcy

Danielle O'Mara

When my parents went away on a short vacation,
I stayed with my older sister, Madeline,
Who works for a real estate office downtown.
I simmered while she nagged me to
Wash the dishes, do the laundry,
    finish my homework.
Nothing I did was good enough for her.
Many evenings ended in heated arguments
    and slammed doors.
When she told me she was bringing a date home,
I decided to surprise her by making dinner.
I used the cookbook but,
The fish was raw,
The spaghetti limp,
The biscuits burnt,
And the poor guy staggered out the door,
    holding his stomach.
I thought my sister would fry me.
She looked at me and said,
"I didn't like him anyway."
We burst out giggling and hugged each other.

Scott Garber

Alex, my brother, we are strangers now.
We share a room, but not much else.
There was a time, I suppose,
When I could have reached out to you,
But I chose not to.
Why?
I didn't want a twin, a mirror of myself.
I didn't want to wear the same clothes
Even though Mom thought it was cute.
I didn't want to go to the same school
Even though the teachers tried not to confuse us.
I wanted a separate identity,
One where I could jump higher, run faster,
Without feeling you were dragging me down.
I am not proud of myself for saying this,
But, Alex, the way you look, dress and act
Embarrasses me.
I look at your imperfections
And hope they are not mine.
I want to outrace the footsteps
I hear following me.

Alex Garber

My brother is so bright
I swear he glows in the dark.
He got all the good genes.
I got all the leftover ones.
He gets all the high grades in school.
I just squeak by.
He gets all the girls.
I stay home a lot.
If I ask him to include me in his plans,
He acts like he's doing me the biggest favor.
Brothers should share more than a last name.
If I am his brother,
Why does he treat me like a stepchild?

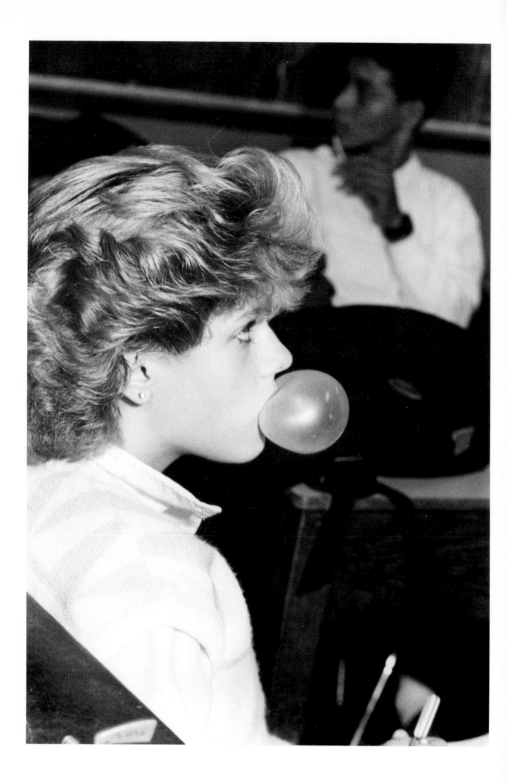

Leigh Hamilton

I have my whole wedding planned out,
What I will wear,
Which church will hold the ceremony,
Where I'll go on my honeymoon.
I have it all planned out.
I'll wear a white silk gown,
Reserve the church for next June
And go to Bermuda for a week.
Then it's on to living happily ever after.
My mother will cry at the reception.
My father will drink too much.
My friends from school will shower me with gifts.
The bridegroom?
Oh, I haven't met him yet.
I have a feeling I will, very soon.
I will tell him to hurry.

Carla Spooner

I can't talk about it,
Least of all to you.
Crying comes much more easily.
You want to talk about what will be?
How we'll be "good friends" and all that crap?
How about what was?
How we were new, excited lovers together?
When I let you into my life,
I didn't see the storm clouds gather.
When I let you get close to me,
I ignored the rain.
What happened to your feelings for me, Billy?
Did you suddenly decide that since I gave you all,
There was nothing more to take?
You sit two seats ahead of me in class,
A matter of a few feet, no doubt.
But the space between us stretches for miles.
I hate you, William Seidman.
I do, I do, I do!

Amanda Butler

Most mothers yell, scream or hyperventilate.
They cajole, wheedle or plead.
They bribe, coerce or threaten.
Not my mother.
She has replaced the telephone
With the refrigerator,
Leaving short, cryptic notes on the door
Held in place by those silly little magnets
Which look like overripe fruits.
A few well-chosen words determine my daily fate.
    "Be home at four – sharp!"
    "Clean up your room – today!"
    "Start dinner – I'll be late."
    "You're grounded – for two weeks."
    "Don't you know what a curfew means?"
    "I just got the phone bill – are you crazy?"
Smart lady, my mother.
There is never a chance to answer back.
"Leave a note," she says
As she flies out the door to work.
It's not the same thing.
Refrigerator conversations leave me cold.

Keith Jordan

My parents wanted me to go
To this very preppy private school,
One that has a manicured lawn out front.
I did.
For two weeks.
It may be one of the best schools around,
But not for me.
The teachers gave too much work.
The older students played practical jokes on me
And I had to wear a school uniform.
Totally embarrassing.
The students came from such rich families,
I swear, they brought three-course meals for lunch.
These kids acted so snotty
That nobody talked to me for a week.
I missed my old friends from the block.
I wished I could go to the local high school,
The one with the torn fence out front.

James Petrie

My parents wanted me to go
To this very ordinary public high school,
One that has a torn fence out front.
I did.
For two weeks.
It may be one of the better schools around,
But not for me.
The teachers gave too little work.
The older students ran wild in the halls
And everything I wore was wrong.
Totally embarrassing.
The students came from such poor families,
I swear, they showed up
Just for the free breakfasts.
These kids acted so rowdy
That I didn't speak to anyone for a week.
I wish my family would move from this block.
I wish I could go to the exclusive prep school,
The one with the manicured lawn out front.

Ian Sinclair

If there is going to be a nuclear winter,
I want to play in the summer sun forever.
If our days on earth are numbered,
I want each remaining one to count.
My friends think I'm crazy
Because I really do think about the Big One.
I've joined peace rallies and protest marches.
I've signed petitions and put up posters.
We already have enough bombs
To blow up the world ten times over.
How many times can you kill a person?
I think my friends are crazy for
Not realizing that seasons change,
That fallout makes for nuclear winter,
And winter kills.

Clint Reynolds

Years ago,
My father would stand over my bed,
The ribbons on his chest
Gleaming in the morning sun.
"Private Reynolds, rise and shine," he'd say,
And I'd reply with a snappy salute, "Yessir!"
This year,
I'm joining the army
To serve and protect my country.
I'd kill anybody ten times over
Who threatens the American way of life.
Next year,
I'll be stationed either here or abroad
With rifle in hand or missile nearby.
No matter where, I'll be ready to
Defend the land I love.
This month,
When I get my diploma from high school,
When I walk proudly to the recruiting office,
I'll remember my father's "rise and shine."
And my reply will be the same as always,
"Yessir!"

Carolyn Warren

In class I often

> Play my Walkman,
> Polish my nails,
> Scribble a few notes,
> Talk to a friend,
> Read *Teen Romance*,
> Put on my makeup,
> Drink my soda,
> Munch on some chips,
> Doodle in my notebook,
> Plan my weekend.

I pass all my tests.
My teachers can't understand it,
But I do.
You just have to have something to do
While you're getting an education.

Isabel Navarro

You want to know what kind of week it's been?
My boyfriend left me for a tramp
Who's beneath him.
Literally.
My best friend borrowed $20 from me and
Gave it to *her* best friend.
My grades for this marking period are so low
I need a crane to lift them up.
My mother filed for separation papers –
From *me*.
The building I live in is falling down so fast
The rats all wear running shoes.
But when I dance onstage,
                    When I dance,
                        When I dance,
My real life slips into the wings
As I leap from the shadows
To soar above
All my pain.

Cynthia Leonard

(After-school Conversation in Room 139)

"Mr. Matthews, how come you're still here?"
"Just marking some papers, Cynthia."
"Mr. Matthews, you busy? Can I talk to you?
I mean, if you're busy, I can come back."
"I'm finished, come on in. Any problem?"
"Well . . . sort of."
"Come on, Cynthia, how serious could it be?
Had a fight with your boyfriend?
Having trouble with math?
I know, you missed your soaps. Right?"
"Er — no, I'll come back, sorry I bothered you."
"No, hold on, bad joke, I'm sorry. What's up?"
"It's just that — Mr. Matthews, please . . ."
"Please what?"
"Mr. Matthews . . . I was downstairs, just
Outside the girls' locker room and this . . .
Guy . . . grabbed me and pulled me down and . . .
Mr. Matthews, please help me.
Please help me!"

Mandy Bailer

(The Lifeguard)

They didn't want me to have this job.
I fought them.
The other lifeguards razzed me.
I ignored them.
People asked, "You a lifeguard?"
"No, a zucchini," I answered them.
Who needs this crap?
Just because I'm a girl
I gotta be a baby-sitter for life?
Or a salesgirl at the mall?
Or a checker at the A & P?
Get away from me with these kinds of jobs.
Today I pulled an old guy from the water.
"Oh, excuse me, sir.
Would you like to see my credentials
While I try to pump the water out of you?"
Gimme a break.
You got any more stupid comments?

Russell Hodges

(The Usher)

Did you see that movie where
The monster ate the alien
Who chopped up the zombie
Who decapitated the creature
Who strangled the werewolf
Who tore apart the giant spider?
I saw it.
Forty-seven times.
And I'm gonna see it forty-seven more times.
It's our biggest hit of the year.
I can hardly wait for the sequel.
If my own life is boring,
A safe, slow boat ride down
A well-marked channel,
Let my movies bring me to the places
Where the wild waves crash against the rocks.
Time for the next show?
Let it roll.
If I can't live it,
At least I'll see it.

Crystal Rowe

(Track Star)

Allthegirlsarebunched
togetheratthestarting
_____ line _____

But

When the gun goes off

I

J

U
M
P

out ahead and
never look back
and
HIT
the

__T__ A __P__ E __

a
WINNER!

Hayes Iverson

(Basketball Star)

The score is tied,
Hands smooth with sweat,
God, let the ball
Fall through the net.
I'm on the line,
Shooting a pair,
First one rolls off,
Black-hole despair.
Ball feels heavy,
Bounce it once more,
Slow breath – let it
Drop for the score.
The ball is up,
Universe waits,
The ball
       d
     r
      o
       p
      s _____
           in,
         69–68!

Lance Perkins

(Football Star)

G	If
5	I
10	run
15	this
20	punt
25	back
30	for
35	a
40	touchdown,
45	do
50	you
45	promise
40	me
35	that
30	the
25	cheering
20	and
15	applause
10	will
5	never
G	stop?

Jennie Tang

At the party honoring my father
I saw all my relatives,
My aunts, my uncles and even some cousins
Newly arrived from Canton.
My parents even let me invite
Three of my favorite teachers.
They did not, however, let me invite David,
Whom they laughingly call the "foreign devil."
David, who makes me breathe funny,
David, who makes me feel loved.
It was a glorious banquet
With twelve different courses.
And I danced happily from table to table,
Lingering to talk with this relative
        or that friend,
Greeting my father's honored guests and
Explaining the wonderful dishes to my teachers.
I would have been happier had my parents
Let me invite David,
David, whose warm smile
Lingers, like a gentle touch,
In my heart.

David Klein

My parents' plans for me include
College,
Medical school,
Internship,
Residency,
Private practice.
Those plans do not include Jennie,
Jennie, who makes me think of
Walks along the shore,
Quick kisses in the movies,
Frisbee-tossing in the park.
"You'll meet the right type of girl,"
  my mother says,
Not making the least attempt to be subtle.
"Somebody with a similar background,"
  my father says,
Not making the least attempt to be understanding.
The thought of Chinese-Jewish grandchildren
Terrifies them.
If I am going to be a doctor
And hold life and death in my hands,
Why can't I take charge of my own life
And hold the hand
Of the girl I love?

Barbara Sutton

What is being rejected?
Only my story for the school lit magazine.
Nothing much in the
Grand design of things, I'm sure.
What is being rejected?
Only hours of thinking, rewriting and typing.
Nothing much in the
Cosmic scope of things, I'm sure.
I'll make jokes, be brave,
Say it doesn't matter, when it does.
Just because there was a little sex in the story,
The faculty advisor told me it was
        "inappropriate."
What does he want —
"Goldilocks and the Three Bears"?
Mr. Barker, one day I'm going to be
A famous writer, you'll see.
I have such wonderful stories in my head.
Why won't you publish them?

Gary Irving

It's hard to explain how I feel.
Some days are up, some down.
Most are just boring, though.
I'm waiting for something to happen,
Like standing at a station, looking for a train.
Every Friday, Harvey and me go bowling.
We're both lousy, but it passes the time.
Afterward, we go for pizza
And talk about how the action'll
    pick up next week,
How we'll get a couple of dates
And really have a good time.
Every week Harvey and me go bowling,
Together and alone.

Harvey Persky

What's on TV these days?
Well, certainly not me.
Policemen who round up all the crooks,
Doctors who cure every patient
And families so close, it's unreal.
Who *are* these people?
Nobody I know, that's for sure.
What's at school these days?
Guys who wear supercool clothes,
Girls who join every activity there is
And teams so close, it's unreal.
Who *are* these people?
Nobody I know, that's for sure.
My only friend in school is Gary.
He's in a lot of my classes,
And we sort of hang out together.
There should be a series about us on TV,
To show what our lives are like.
Only it probably would be as interesting as
A blank screen.

Michelle Church

I told Faith I didn't want to go
To the movies with her anymore.
All she does is run away from her problems.
Besides, there are too many creeps there
In the afternoon.
I'd rather rush home from school
And watch my soaps.
Rapes, abortions, murders – I love it!
I can tell you anything about any character,
Who they slept with, who they want to sleep with.
I hate my life because nothing happens to it.
Last week our house was robbed
While I was watching my favorite program.
I never heard a thing.
Our whole house was turned upside down.
The police came;
My mother cried;
My father screamed;
I was bored by the whole thing.

Mary Louise Donahue

The only way I would follow God was if
He played in a rock 'n' roll band.
How dare I say that, Mom?
Easy.
I'm sick of your rules
Masquerading as good advice:
Go to church,
Go to school,
Do this,
Do that.
I'm sick of you always telling me what to do,
And who to associate with.
I know Monica moved out of her house
And is *actually* living with someone.
Does that mean I should stop seeing her?
She is my friend, and I accept her.
Yes, I'm still friendly with Diana.
No, I don't keep secret diaries, why do you ask?
My friends accept me for who I am.
You don't.
If they aren't good enough for you, Mom,
Then perhaps neither am I.

Rachel Ferrara

More than anything, I want to be an actress.
My first part was as a cabbage
    in the first grade.
My father used to take off work
    just to see me perform.
He would applaud wildly,
Yelling ''Bravo, bravo'' over and over again.
All through elementary school,
    he never missed a show.
In junior high he came less frequently,
But I could still hear his bravo
    from the rear of the auditorium.
Now in high school, I hardly see him at all.
He says I'm well on my way.
I am too embarrassed
    to ask for the encouragement
I still need.
But maybe,
He's just lost interest in the theater
Or in me.

Brian Nichols

I can't tell you exactly when love begins,
A soft look,
A shared joke,
An agreement on which
Teachers,
Rock bands,
Friends
Are great and which ones
Are not.
Not knowing what to say, I drew
Little pictures for Judy of
Teachers,
Rock bands,
Friends
And sought in her approving eyes a love
That was growing, but never stated by me.
It's so hard to communicate what you feel inside.
She must have grown tired of my evasions,
For when I didn't say
What should have been said next
She killed the blossom.
I can tell you exactly when love ends.

Tina DeMarco

When I was a little girl,
I would take my mother's fashion magazines
And hide them under my pillow.
Then, when my family thought I was asleep,
I'd read them by the hazy glow of my night-light.
Every model's face was my own.
Every splash of color looked good on me.
Older now, I've run into a few problems.
After school, as I make the rounds
Of studios and agencies, I hear,
"You're too tall."
"You're not what we have in mind."
"You're very short on professional experience."
Becoming a model is not as easy as it looks.
Now, late at night, I sit in front
     of my makeup mirror,
Trying out new shades and glosses,
And wonder if the girl in the fashion magazine
Will ever be me.

Neil Winningham

"Two out, bottom of the ninth,
     men on first and third."
               My father died three years ago.
               That's his picture on my desk.
               I know he looks kinda funny,
               I mean, a man dressed in a suit
               Wearing a baseball cap.
"Strike one."
               When I was five,
               He'd take me to lots of games,
               Stuff me with candy and
               Describe all the action on the field.
               I'd fall asleep in his arms,
               Listening to the play-by-play.
               He'd tilt the cap over my eyes
               To shield me from the sun.
"Strike two."
               Death ended his life
               Before the ninth inning.
               It did not end my love.
               I sit at my desk, do my homework
               And listen to the ball game.
               I hear the announcer's voice
               Describing all the action.
               It's not his voice I hear,
               But one I heard many years ago.
"The batter swings — this one's out of here, folks!
     Tie score! We're going into extra innings."
Oh, Daddy . . .

Meredith Piersall

(Senior Trip)

Some people are born to
Paint, run, write or play the piano.
I was born to shop.
I love to run through department store aisles
And yell, "Charge!"
Actually, I must buy a new outfit
For the senior trip.
Something flashy, not trashy,
Something that might catch Howie's attention,
If I can ever pry him loose from Wendy, that is.
I have to be subtle, yet fairly obvious about it.
I don't want a whole big scene on the bus
    with Wendy.
Oh, relationships, even new ones, are so difficult,
And they unravel so quickly.
Shopping is much easier.
You select what you want off the rack,
And if you don't like it,
You return the merchandise.
No harm done.
With relationships,
There are always strings attached.

Howie Bystrom

(Senior Trip — The Amusement Park)

Somewhere between
The Flume Ride and the Bumper Cars
I lost my love.
She didn't like getting wet
Nor did she like getting racked up on the turns.
When I suggested the Wild Bobsled Ride,
She stopped, looked at me sharply
And said with unintended irony,
"Howie, we travel in different circles. Grow up!"
When she walked off toward the midway,
I tried to win her back with
Teddy bears and cotton candy.
But even if I had a voice
As convincing as a sideshow barker's
It would not change the fact that
She has outgrown
All the rides,
All the games,
And me.

Wendy Tarloff

(Senior Trip — The Amusement Park)

Somewhere between
The Flume Ride and the Bumper Cars
I dropped Howie.
I hadn't planned on it;
I didn't mean to be cruel.
But when he suggested one more
Loud, lurching ride, it seemed a proper metaphor
For a relationship that was going nowhere
But in circles.
I told him quite clearly
That we were through,
That I was tired of his horsing around,
Tired of his macho mentality.
He called me names that were definitely juvenile.
I think I'll take a walk on over
To the Tunnel of Love.
You never know who you might meet there,
Someone new,
Someone cute,
Someone grown-up enough to enjoy a
Slow, easy ride to maturity.

Kurt Benoit

(Senior Trip – The Hotel)

"Come to my window at two a.m.,"
She said softly.
"Come to me by moonlight."
After the amusement park, after dinner
I met a girl from another school
Who was a vision previously seen
Only in my dreams.
"Come to me by moonlight."
You bet.
Later, just as I had figured out
Which window was hers
A huge hand grabbed me.
"What are you doing?"
My teacher snarled at me.
"Curfew was an hour ago."
"Just visiting," I said,
Trying to charm my way out of trouble.
"These girls are thirteen years old,
From a religious school.
Are you crazy?" he yelled.
"Thirteen?" I said, shaking my head.
"I thought she was just short."
Bet Romeo never had it so rough.

Beth Rossiter . . . and . . .

(Couple 1 – Prom)

Douglas,
You'd be a lot better off
If I were your friend again,
Instead of your date for the prom.
As friends, we used to talk a lot to each other,
Share secrets, trade dirt and exchange homework.
Now we can't seem to keep our hands off
     each other
And I'm not so sure we're any closer.
Your love has changed me into a
Possessive, vulnerable woman.
I'm not sure I like the change.
Oh, don't get me wrong –
I think you're a tender and delightful lover.
My one and only Douglas, sweet Douglas.
And yet I wonder if a
Couple of moments of passion are
Equal to the beauty of a deep friendship?
Don't hold me so close, Dougie, as we dance.
I'd like to remember the good times
Before we got so damn
Serious.

. . . *Douglas Kearny*

Beth,
I know I look ridiculous
In this tux that doesn't quite fit.
I know that the corsage I got for you
Doesn't quite match your dress.
I know that the band forgot
About my request to play our special song.
I know that my dancing leaves
A lot to be desired.
But most of all,
I know I want to say in symbols
What I can't say in words,
That I love you.
I have never said, "I love you"
To anyone before.
I will never say, "I love you"
To anyone but you.
So hold me close, Beth, as we dance.
I'd like to remember the good times,
The good times which I hope will last
Forever.

Sharon Vail . . . and . . .

(Couple 2 – Prom)

Because I wanted life in the fast lane,
I got thrown off-track.
Because I wanted to experience it all,
I am driving out of control.
I got Ronnie here for my date,
Mr. High School, Mr. Wonderful.
He's so ice-smooth he slides across the floor.
I really wanted to go to the prom with Douglas,
But he was already taken
By Beth, who was smart enough to see
That nice is better than ice.
(I wonder if she's sleeping with him.
Naah, she's too goody-goody for that stuff.)
Maybe I should shift gears
And slow down a bit.
I might get more mileage
Out of my relationships that way.
"Hey, Ronnie, could you ask them
To play a ballad?
Something nice and easy."

. . . Ronnie Evans

You see this prom?
Who do you think arranged it all?
I got the hall.
I got the flowers.
I got the band.
Everything.
For the best price.
All night long, people have been coming up to me
And telling me how wonderful the prom is.
Hey, what can I tell you,
I'm a talented guy.
Forget about college,
I'm going straight into business
And make my millions.
Sharon,
I ain't got time to dance now.
Gotta run.
Gotta check out some glitch
In the seating arrangements.
Catch you later.

Angelina Falco . . . and . . .

(Couple 3 – Prom)

I was twelve when my sister
Went to her high school prom.
I sat on her bed and
Asked her a thousand questions.
She wore a long blue dress
With spaghetti straps.
She said that when I was older
I could wear that dress.
Now I'm a senior too.
No one has asked me to the prom.
I don't think anybody will –
It's too late.
I'll never have the chance
To wear that blue dress.
I sometimes take it out of her closet,
Press it to my body,
Twirl around the room
And catch a look at my elegant self.
Then I pretend that my date is
Just about to ring the front-door bell.

. . . *Mario Benedetto*

From my friend Joey:
 "She's a loser, a dog, a definite bow-wow."
From my friend Frankie:
 "She has the sex appeal of sludge."
From my friend Victor:
 "Angelina? You've got to be kidding."
Listening to friends,
Hearing their cheap shots,
I forgot to listen to my own voice,
Which I found while talking to Angelina.
I decided to hell with my friends
And asked Angelina to the prom.
Even though I asked her at the
Last possible moment,
She said yes.
OK, so she doesn't look like a Hollywood star,
But, then again, neither do I.
She makes me laugh.
She understands the way I feel.
She looks elegant in that long blue dress.
And I like her!
Maybe Angie is not the great fireworks explosion
In my life, but I'd rather bask
In the warm glow of her candle-lit face
Than stand with you guys on the outside
 in the dark,
Dumping on every female in sight.
You hear me, guys?

Min Trang

(Graduation)

Four years ago I walk through the jungles
To find boat which take me to America.
I left behind father and two small brother.
Today I walk down the graduation aisles
To find new life in America.
I leave behind my boyhood forever.
I will go to university,
Work hard and study computers.
Then to find good job to bring
Rest of my family over.
All my days in America been wonderful,
But this is most wonderful day of all.
I get my high school diploma,
A great honor.
I write letters to my father
Telling him of my progress.
I not heard from him in over one year.
I hope he is alive.

Carlos Rodriguez

(Graduation)

Father Thomas,
It has been two months since my last confession.
I know I haven't been to church much lately,
But on the eve of my graduation
I wanted to tell you how much I owe you.
I was a helpless mess, all mixed up.
You said I was going through changes.
I said my friends all left me flat.
You said to rely on my own family.
I wanted to run away from all my problems.
You showed me the difference between
Running to and running from.
But you want to know the best thing
You ever said to me?
You said, "If you don't know what you want,
Don't throw away what you have."
You remember telling me that?
If the church is what I have,
If the church is my rock,
You are the fisherman atop that rock
Who reeled me in.
Thank you, Father.

Arlene Lasky

(Graduation)

I mean, let's get this graduation over with, OK?
These speeches are boring,
The band is off-key
And nobody knows the alma mater anyway.
This is a joke.
I'm sweating here under this cap and gown.
I don't really care if the tassel goes
From right to left or left to right.
Hey, this graduation is not for me.
It's for my parents, uncles and aunts,
Who all want to shake my hand or hug me.
Hey, you're crushing me.
Can't you just take pictures like normal people?
If I hear one more time
That my future is ahead of me,
I'll barf right here in the aisle.
For four years this school has done nothing but
Hassle me about grades, attendance and attitude.
But they can't get me now,
I'm graduating, man.
It's time to party!

Jessica Berg

(Graduation)

It's too easy to
    Walk away,
    Sit down,
    Get over.
It's too easy to be
    Cynical,
    Cool,
    Miserable.
It's too easy to turn
    A deaf ear,
    A cold heart,
    A silent voice.
It's too easy to doubt
    Your chances,
    Your future,
    Yourself.
And I never liked nor took the easy way out.
So, in a few minutes when they call my name
To come up for the diploma I earned,
I will walk with pride up to the stage.
Easily.

Cecilia Dowling

(One Year Later)

Dear Mr. Henderson,
    I don't know exactly
Why I'm writing this letter.
You probably don't remember me,
But I remember everything you said,
Even though that was more than a year ago.
You were my favorite teacher.
You saw past my poor grades
And spotty attendance
And made me think I had value,
Substance even.
No, I didn't go to college.
I didn't even finish
The beauty school I went to.
I tried to learn makeup,
But all I learned was that no matter
What paint or brushes I used
I couldn't cover the blemishes
I saw in myself.
"It's not as bad as all that, Cecilia,"
You'd probably say.
No, it isn't.
I hear your words in my head
And in my heart, even now.
Why am I writing you this letter?
Because I want you to know
You mattered in my life – you still do.
                Love, C.

Todd Michaels

(One Year Later)

If I serve one more piece of chicken,
I'll become a permanent vegetarian.
If one more customer asks me
If the biscuits are fresh,
I'll bounce one off his head.
Even school was better than this place.
Not by much, though.
Why did I take this job?
To gain valuable work experience?
To learn corporate structure?
To earn money for college?
Naah!
I wanted to meet the cute girls
Who work in the offices across the street.
So what if they're a couple of years older
Than me?
I don't care.
When I look down at the breasts and legs I serve,
You can be sure it's not the chicken
I'm thinking about!

Mary Beth Collier

(One Year Later)

Your order, miss?
Oh, it's you.
Haven't seen you since high school.
How ya been?
That's good. Me?
All right, I guess.
My boss asked me to work full-time.
Couldn't say no, could I?
You're right, I should be in college now.
That's right, I love English lit,
Especially the poets like Browning, Jonson,
Wordsworth and Milton.
You have a good memory.
I can't go to school at night
Because I don't have my high school diploma.
Failed math in my last term.
I begged Griswald to pass me,
But he wouldn't do it.
I'd like to fry him on the griddle.
But I'm OK, really I am.
"They also serve who only stand and wait."
Milton wrote that —
I think especially for me.
Was that a tuna on rye?

Heather Yarnell

(One Year Later)

I really don't have time to breathe.
Five finals to study for
Plus a term paper that's just a mess
Of index cards right now.
I didn't think college would be a breeze,
But nobody told me it would be *this* rough.
I spend all week reading and studying
And when the weekend comes
All I want to do is sleep.
Alone.
I hate to admit it, but I miss high school.
Can you believe that?
Me, who couldn't wait to graduate,
Me, who couldn't get out
Of my parents' house fast enough.
College is a job — with plenty of overtime.
High school was a kid's game
Where days played tag with one another,
Where friendships, loves and worries
Started and stopped and started again.
I wonder where Cecilia is now
And what Mary Beth is doing.
Hey, what's with this nostalgia trip?
I really don't have time to breathe.

Brandon Dale

(One Year Later –
High School Reunion Questionnaire)

Name: Brandon Dale
Graduation Date: Last year
Sex: Sometimes (only kidding) male
Things you miss about high school:
>   My friends, mostly; one or two teachers,
>   Hangin' out, the girls (most of them),
>   Friday night parties

Things you don't miss about high school:
>   My enemies, mostly; one or two teachers,
>   Homework, snotty girls, report cards,
>   Required gym, detention

Things you would do differently
> if you were in high school again:
>   Work a little harder perhaps,
>   Not cut out, apply myself more,
>   Try out for one of the teams,
>   Cut out smoking, listen more,
>   Stick with one girl for a while

Best subject:
>   None of them; pretty much all the same

Worst subject:
>   See above

Present occupation:
>   Work in a garage on Main on the weekends

Choice of date for this reunion:
>   I don't care, I got plenty of time.

Miguel DeVega

(One Year Later)

In school I gave everybody trouble.
My parents, my teachers, but most of all
Mr. Davenport, the vice-principal.
I'd put shaving cream on his car windows.
He'd suspend me.
I'd cut out of class.
He'd have my mother up to school in a flash.
I'd start food fights in the cafeteria.
He'd give me detention for weeks.
"DeVega," he'd say, "you again?
I have serious doubts about your future."
After just squeezing through high school,
And after figuring I had screwed up everything,
I did a complete about-face and joined the army.
No sweat. It was just like school.
Rules are rules anywhere.
I survived basic and even went to gunnery school.
Before being shipped overseas, I dropped by
        the old school, in uniform.
"DeVega," Mr. Davenport said, stopping
        me in the hall, "you again?"
He looked at me squarely for a few seconds
Before adding, "I don't have any doubts
        about your future."
Then he gave me a very military salute,
Which I returned.
It was the best moment I ever had in high school,
Even if it came a year late.